For Johanna
M. W.

For Leon
"Magic with Flowers"
C. A.

Text copyright © 1999 by Martin Waddell
Illustrations copyright © 1999 by Camilla Ashforth

First U.S. edition 1999
Library of Congress Cataloging-in-Publication Data

Waddell, Martin.
Who do you love? / Martin Waddell ; illustrated by Camilla Ashforth.—1st U.S. ed.
p.   cm.
Summary: At bedtime a mother cat and her kitten Holly play the game
"Who Do You Love?" and Holly describes everyone she loves and her reasons for doing so.
ISBN 0-7636-0586-7
[1. Cats—Fiction. 2. Love—Fiction. 3. Bedtime—Fiction.]
I. Ashforth, Camilla, ill. II. Title.
PZ7.W1137Wj   1999
[E]—dc21   98-3455

2 4 6 8 10 9 7 5 3 1

Printed in Hong Kong

This book was typeset in Granjon.
The pictures were done in watercolor and pencil.

Candlewick Press
2067 Massachusetts Avenue
Cambridge, Massachusetts 02140

WHO DO YOU LOVE?

Martin Waddell

illustrated by Camilla Ashforth

CANDLEWICK PRESS
CAMBRIDGE, MASSACHUSETTS

Holly played on the hillside each night until Mama called her in for supper. "Night-night!" Holly said. "Night-night, Holly!" called her friends, and Holly went in.

"Bedtime now, Holly!" said Mama,
when they had finished their supper.
"I want to play our go-to-bed
game!" Holly said.
"Bed first, then the game,"
Mama said.
"I want to play while I'm getting
ready for bed," Holly said.
And Mama started the game.

"Who do you love, Holly?"
asked Mama.

"I love Grandpa," Holly said.

"He takes me for walks in the woods,
and he makes dandelion clocks
for me. And I hide away where he
can't see me. He says, 'Where are
you, Holly?' Then I jump out
and shout **BOO!**"

"Poor Grandpa!" said Mama.

"Now ask me again!" Holly said.

"Who do you love?" asked Mama.

"Let me think!" Holly said.

"I love Grandma because she makes big cakes at her house. She stirs the batter, and I put the cherries on top. Then I lick the spoon. Grandma makes the best cakes in the woods."

"You'll get fat eating cakes," said Mama.

"I don't care!" Holly said. "I like Grandma's cakes."

Mama looked for the towel, but Holly

wanted more of the game.

"Ask me who I love," Holly said.

"Ask me again!"

"Who do you love?" asked Mama.

"I love Arthur," said Holly.

"I love Arthur because he is my brother. He lets me ride his bike. Sometimes I ride down the hill, and then I fall off at the bottom. Arthur says that's how you learn to ride bikes."

"I see!" said Mama.

"Ask me some more!"
Holly said.

"Who do you love?" asked Mama.

"I love Pa because he is my Pa,"
Holly said. "He tells me stories all
about my adventures."

"What sort of adventures?"
asked Mama.

"I was a princess and I lived
in a castle with Arthur. One day
there was a dragon, and Arthur didn't
know what to do. I got some water
and poured it all over the dragon
and put his fire out. Pa says I saved
Arthur, and I made the dragon
my friend," Holly said.

"Who else do you love?"
   asked Mama.

"I think that's everyone now,"
   Holly said.

"You've left someone out!"
   said Mama.
   It was the part of the game that
   Holly liked best.

"Ask me again!" Holly said.

"Who do you love, Holly?"
   asked Mama.

"I love . . . old Postman
Cat because he brings us
our letters," Holly said.
"Just old Postman Cat?"
asked Mama.

"I love . . .
Cousin Ollie
who comes every
Sunday," Holly said.
"I love Cousin Ollie a lot!"

"I love . . .
  the cat with the hat
  that we met yesterday
  in the woods,"
Holly said.

"I love . . .
  the three kittens
  who roll down
  the hill,"
Holly said.

"I think I might cry!" sighed Mama.

"Don't cry, Mama," Holly said.

"You just have to ask me again."

"Who do you love, Holly?"
 asked Mama.

"I love you," said Holly.

"And I love you too," Mama said.

"You know that I do."

Mama hugged Holly and put her to bed,

and that was the end of the

go-to-bed game.